Pumpkin Spiced Love

Jacqueline Carmine

Content Warnings

Graphic Sexual Content

Bondage

Unprotected Sex

Breeding Kink

Primal Play

Mask Kink

Religious Role Play (Priest/Nun)

Breath Play

Verbal Degradation (Whore/Slut Etc.)

Spanking (Mentioned)

Grave Desecration

JACQUELINE CARMINE

Emma

"Shut the fuck up and take that dick like a good girl." Andrew breathes against the arch of my neck right before he leans back to look at where his cock is pounding into me. The first words he has ever spoken to me make me impossibly wetter as he continues his invasion of my body. His tattooed hand leaves my breast and wraps around the hollow of my throat. A warm choker of roses and thorns.

"My hand looks so good around your neck baby girl." He says with a firm squeeze.

Warmth spreads through my core as he applies pressure to my throat at the same time as he begins rubbing my clit in smooth fast circles.

"I'm so close." I whimper when he lets go of my neck to grab my thigh and lift it high on his hip, "Don't stop. Please God don't stop."

His eyes hold a feral gleam behind the mask's eye cutouts. The blue eyes stand out from the white mask in the shape of a shocked ghost. He had answered the door silently and naked except for the mask just as we had agreed on the app. If I had known the things he would say I never would have chained his voice for even a moment.

"I'll never let you go now." He promises in a raspy voice. Beads of sweat roll down his chest and I feel the bizarre urge to trace their path with my tongue.

"Mark me." I order as he resumes circling my clit.

His hips begin to stutter when I go over the edge arching my back and thrusting my breasts forward. He jerks back pulling his cock out while my walls are still spasming with the aftershocks of my orgasm. He strokes his cock as he paints my belly and mound with thick ropes of his seed. For just a moment I regret not asking him to come inside me. I'm on birth control and we've both been tested. It was something we discussed before I even bought my plane ticket.

Andrew sits back on his heels as we both take a moment to catch our breath.

Downloading the SoulConnect app on my phone was a whim. Sharing all my kinks that I was too embarrassed to tell any previous boyfriend about with a stranger was easy. Meeting a stranger to have sex and fulfill those desires was crazy and scary. Coming to his cabin in the mountains without vetting him was foolish. He could be a serial killer ready to carve me up and feed me to the local wolves. A little risk and danger had set the perfect mood for my mask kink.

"Cool if I take this off now?" Andrew asks.

I nod and watch as he pulls the rubber mask off his sweaty face. His dark hair falls in loose damp curls over his ears, and he has a scattering of freckles over his nose. His blue eyes meet mine and it feels like my breath is knocked out of me.

I need to leave before I beg him to kiss me. We had consented to a single encounter with no strings. It is time for me to go.

As I begin to gather my things Andrew watches me with a sheepish expression. Just as I slip back into my dress, he finally breaks the silence.

"Feel free to say no but would you like to get breakfast with me?" He asks as he grabs his dark wash jeans and pulls them on.

He's not looking at me and for a moment I fear it's a pity invite but then I see his Adam's apple bobbing nervously as he waits for my answer.

"I'd love some waffles." I say with a shy smile.

I've always been the safe bet. The girl the parents like and invite to holidays but never the woman who ignites a man's darkest desires. Plain boring and vanilla until Andrew and I clicked together on the dating app.

Now I'm going to have breakfast with a man whose face I didn't see until *after* we had sex. A man who readily agreed to wear a mask and choke me while he fucked me.

"There's a little diner up the road. Looks awful but the food is phenomenal." Andrew says as he slips a T-shirt over his head and grabs a pair of black framed glasses off the side table.

"I'm not local so I'll take your word for it." I tell him as he leads me outside his cabin. I go to hop in my car, but he stops me with a hand on my arm.

"Unless that's all-wheel drive you might want to ride with me." He says gesturing at his old square bodied truck.

My hesitancy to leave my car behind is telling and he's quick to explain.

"It's a little way up the mountain on the ridge. There is a small town there and the road isn't paved and we're expecting rain. You can take your car but if it gets stuck, I'll have to bring you down in my truck and then you'll have to wait for a tow truck. I don't have the equipment to pull you out of the mud much less tow you down the mountain." He says rubbing the back of his neck.

I appreciate the explanation, but the car is a level of security I need. Knowing I can leave at any time if I'm uncomfortable or don't feel safe isn't a luxury I want to give up.

"I'll follow you up and I'll be careful." I tell him before I climb into the driver seat of my rental car.

He waits for me to get settled and then he closes the door for me. It's a little bit more than just up the road but when we pull into a gravel parking lot beside a rundown little shack of a diner my stomach is rumbling and I'm ready for food.

He opens my door and holds my hand as we enter the diner.

"Morning Andrew." A woman old enough to be my grandmother greets him before the door closes behind us.

"Hello Wendy. Dave. This is Emma." He calls over to the counter where she is ringing up a large man in a flannel shirt and dirty jeans.

They both turn to look at me and I give a little wave as Andrew leads me to a booth by the windows.

"Small town." He says before I can ask.

Coming from a city where I can never be alone outside my apartment but surrounded by strangers, I feel a sense of longing. To know everyone and have everyone know me.

"Finally use that mail order bride website the men were telling you about huh?" Wendy asks when she comes over to take our order.

"No!" Andrew shouts immediately, "She's just my date, not my wife." His face flushed red in embarrassment.

The woman and I share a look before I order a stack of waffles and sweet tea. Andrew orders an omelet and coffee.

"So, mail order bride?" I ask when she walks away.

"Small town, no tiny town." He says rubbing his temples and avoiding my gaze. "Few women live up here and it's difficult to meet anyone when you work for a logging company or live off grid. A lot of the mountain men around here have to send off for wives just to have a chance at love."

"But not you." I reply.

"I'm not marrying a stranger." He replies as Wendy brings our food over. She's gone in a blink without a word and when I'm sure she's out of earshot I can't help but tease him.

"Worried you'll end up married to an axe murderer?"

"No. I'm worried she'll take one look at a man like Dave and trade up." He replies between bites.

"Dave seemed nice." I say.

"He doesn't know what STFUATTDLAGG means." Andrew says dismissively.

"I'm sure I could teach him." I needle him a bit further. Jealousy has never been a turn on, but the possessiveness Andrew is displaying has me squirming in my seat and rubbing my thighs together.

"Stop it before I spank you in front of everyone." He orders locking his blue eyes with mine.

A part of me wants to continue and see if he is bluffing but another part just wants to drag him back to bed for round two.

"Have I been a bad girl?" I ask just as he takes a bite of his omelet.

Watching him choke shouldn't be a turn on, but it is when I'm the reason he forgot how to swallow.

"I guess you'll just have to punish me after breakfast." I add playing with the strap of my dress as he chugs his coffee.

"You little brat." He growls as I turn my attention to my waffles.

They are thick and coated with a heavy layer of butter on top. I pour a thick maple syrup over them until it drips down the sides of the stack and pools on the plate. As Andrew devours his omelet, I take small, measured bites of sweet fluffy heaven.

He watches me over the rim of the coffee mug emblazoned with the diner's logo as I slowly work my way through the stack. Rain begins pelting the diner's windows and the blue sky has gone grey.

"You can try to drag this out all you want but you're still going to be punished when we get home." He mutters as I finish up.

"It's called table manners." I reply with a raised eyebrow as I place my knife and fork in a cross on my plate.

I try to split the check, but he waves me off when I go for my wallet. Wendy tosses me a wink as we leave and shouts, "Look forward to seeing you around the ridge, Emma!" before the door closes behind us.

I smile and catch her eye through the glass door. I wave goodbye before we dash through the heavy rain to my car.

"I'll lead you down. Keep my taillights in view and if you lose visibility stop. More than one person has gone over the edge of the mountain in the rain." Andrew says as he opens my door so I can slide into my car.

I nod unable to vocalize my thoughts in any kind of coherent manner. I want this to be more than teasing. I want to continue flirting with this kind and chivalrous man.

Following him back to his house is slower with my windshield wipers barely able to keep up with the rain. More than once I follow him to ride the middle of the gravel road when deep ruts have filled with muddy water on the sides of the road. We passed no one on our way down and when we reached his cabin, I breathed a sigh of relief. I thought he was exaggerating but I had peaked over the guard rail as we drove down, and the steep drop coupled with my car's poor traction had stolen my breath.

Climbing out of my car before Andrew could make his way over to me, I ran to the front porch. Heavy steps pound against the wet ground right behind me and I whirl around as I reach the front door only for him to pick me up by my waist and pin me to the mahogany door.

His mouth slams against mine and all I can feel is the smooth glide of his wet skin on mine. I grab twin handfuls of his hair even as my legs wrap around his waist, my thighs squeezing him as tight as they can. Fighting to get closer I wiggle until I can feel his cock pressed to the warm heat between my legs. The rough denim brushing against the thin gusset of my panties.

He thrusts his hips at the same time as his tongue enters my mouth. Rough and solid, his kiss sets me alight with fiery passion. Breaking our kiss to latch onto my neck I moan as warm tingles spread from where his teeth drag against my sensitive arch to the tips of my breasts.

"Hold on." Andrew orders as he shifts my weight to his left hand and frees his other to open the door. Lingering heat from this morning eases the chill from the rain as he carries us into the cabin slamming the door behind us.

Clutching his firm shoulders, I cling to him as his long strides carry us through the house. I reach down his back to grab the hem of his shirt and begin pulling it up over his head as we enter the bedroom.

He bumps the dresser when I whip the shirt over his head, and he chuckles at my eagerness. It's only been a few hours since we had sex, but this feels urgent. The teasing has built up tension that only Andrew can ease.

I drag my nails down his smooth chest as our lips press together soft and solid at once. Stumbling towards the bed he lets me pull him down, never breaking our kiss. I wiggle to line up our hips even as he grinds down to meet me.

Pulling back for a moment, Andrew shoves the top of my dress down to bare my breasts and I slip the straps off my arms to help him. Mouth latching onto one peaked nipple he thrusts against my core as I moan. Nails scratching his scalp and back, anywhere I can get a grip all I can do is lay back and claw as he drags a rough tongue against my sensitive nipple. His free hand captures its twin rubbing a callous thumb against the nub as his tongue swirls around the other.

"Andrew, stop teasing." I cry as the heat between my legs continues to rise. I can feel my arousal spreading. My panties are damp and likely my dress as well.

I feel his chuckle before I hear it.

"Only good girls get to come on my cock." He says after releasing my nipple with a pop.

"No." I beg as he switches sides. Warmth pools low in my belly and my legs tingle as he continues to play with my nipples, teasing me higher and higher until I plunge off the cliff in a wave of ecstasy.

My pussy clenches on air and I moan at the lack of his cock, his fingers, *anything* to fill it.

Not all orgasms are created equal and if he doesn't get his cock into me before the next one, I might just become the axe murderer I feared meeting in the mountains.

"Andrew." I growl after he palms both of my breasts and squishes them together. He alternates licking one hardened peak and then the other.

"You don't give the orders in this bed, Emma." Andrew says before he lets go of my breasts and slides off the bed to kneel between my legs. My hands grip the bed spread as he palms my thighs spreading my legs wide to accommodate the broad expanse of his shoulders.

He pushes the skirt of my dress up until the entire garment is bunched around my waist. My blue panties slide down my legs and just when I think he's going to remove his jeans and give me what I've damn near begged for his tongue flicks my clit.

Warm wet tongue tracing my slit he meanders for a bit before thrusting his tongue inside me as far as it will go. Plunging deep and stroking my walls his grip on my thighs is sure to leave bruises even as his tongue paints me. When he does remove his tongue, I'm a quivering mess on the edge of a second orgasm and when he turns his attention back to my clit I shake and moan as I crest the edge again.

But he doesn't stop there. He gives me no quarter as his tongue laps at my clit. He doesn't let me move even as I instinctively try to wiggle away from the contact on my oversensitive nub. Lips latch onto my clit forming a tight seal and as he sucks on the tight bud it's everything I can do not to scream.

"I-I need you." I moan as my hips flex against his

hold, back arching and teeth grinding as electricity runs down my veins. My heartbeat is loud in my ears, and I don't hear his response as he finally relinquishes his hold.

I watch in a daze as he unbuttons his jeans and slides the denim and his boxers off in one go. His gaze is hungry, and I can't look away from the intensity. He looks at me like he knows every part of me. This has turned into far more than a hookup for either of us.

As he crawls back onto the bed, I reach for him, and he comes readily into my arms. Our kiss is messy in the best ways. I taste my arousal on his lips and tongue as he lines up the head of his cock with my entrance.

"Guess I'm a good girl now." I mumble as he slides inside of me.

"So, fucking good," He growls thrusting slowly, "A good girl who knows just how to take me."

"Like this?" I ask with a mumble as I squeeze my muscles around his girth. His eyes go wide with shock, and I can't help the giggle that bubbles up.

"You're gonna pay, Emma." He slams into me brushing my clit with his pelvic bone. Again, and again his hips slam against mine pushing us up the bed with the force.

Just as I go to ask if he prefers cash or a card his hand covers my mouth squeezing my lips together.

"Mpmh." Is all I can get out around his palm. His blue

eyes sparkle with mirth even as his eyebrows furrow on his brow. Grumpy but playful.

"Look at you." He leans back to look at where our bodies are joined, "You look so good when you're sucking my cock inside of you."

Bending over me changes his angle and suddenly the head of his cock is hitting the perfect spot making me gasp beneath his palm. Breathless I almost don't hear his next words.

"It's like you were made for me." He whispers into my ear, and I come, screaming against his hand. I feel him pull out at the last second bathing me in his seed again as my joints stiffen and lock as my vision goes dark.

I wake moments or minutes later underneath the covers sprawled across Andrew's bare chest.

"There you are." He says fondly realizing I'm awake, "How was your nap?"

A slap to his chest just makes it rumble with laughter under my head.

"My car is stuck." I announce without a hint of guile.

"You haven't checked-" Andrew begins to brush me off when he stops midsentence realization hitting him and making his blue eyes shine bright with hope. "Oh."

"Oh." I repeat with a nod.

"You'll stay the weekend?" Andrew asks.

"If that's okay." I reply, "I can reschedule my flight."

"More than okay." He replies pulling me in for a kiss, "It's perfect."

It's impulsive and crazy but I'm done playing it safe. You'll never hit a home run sitting on the bench and I've finally found something worth stepping up to the plate. His eyes grab my attention when we separate, the pupils dilated to the point that they're beginning to swallow the blue.

"Do we-" He stops, "Can we-" he attempts before shaking his head.

I wait for him to gather his thoughts.

"Delete our profiles?" He asks after a moment.

"Well, I don't know about you, but I don't want other women messaging my boyfriend trying to hook up with him."

"A yes would suffice."

"Too boring."

"Such a brat." He says before swatting my ass.

The slight sting reminds me that he still hasn't made good on his threat.

"You never did give me that spanking."

Andrew

I knew it before I took her to *Lenny's*. Emma is perfect. Not literally. She's a normal human woman with quirks and imperfections. To anyone else looking in this would look like a fleeting infatuation. But in a very palpable and tangible way I know she's mine. This is more than a crush or a fling. This is my forever, and I need to handle this with care, or I will ruin the best thing that's ever happened to me.

I need to play it cool.

"Want to go to the Halloween festival later?" I ask as I rub a hand up her bare back.

Later I'm going to give her that spanking...and so much more. But for now, I need time to recover, and I need to show her the town. Let her fall in love with the tiny mountain town before she falls in love with me.

"Hell yes!" She shouts, "Are you freaking serious? Do they have a haunted house?"

She begins rambling, not waiting for me to answer any of her questions, excitement pouring off her in waves.

"It's my favorite holiday. I always try to hit as many

haunted houses and trails as I can every year. My friends are *sick* of going with me."

"I don't know if they have a haunted house." I tell her, thinking about how the festival is more about face painting and pumpkin carving.

I see the disappointment dim her smile and I rush to add, "But there is a creepy graveyard."

"Aren't all graveyards creepy?" She retorts with her smile returning in full bloom.

"No, some are downright fancy with their neat little rows and their manicured lawns."

"Tell me more." She whispers into my ear as her hand paints lazy circles on my chest.

Looking down and noticing the gleam in her eye I don't fight my smirk. Bending the arm not holding her close I put my hand behind my head and let her see my bicep flex. She doesn't make it obvious that she notices but I see her pupils dilate.

"It's old, some of the gravestones can't be read they're so faded. The entire thing is overgrown with creeping vines and wildflowers. Some of the locals say they can hear the spirits whispering late at night." I say letting my voice go lower until it sounds downright sinister.

"You're pulling my leg." She says frowning.

"Nope." I say before flicking her scrunched up nose with the tip of my finger, "I'll show you tonight and let you see for yourself."

My answer seems to reassure her, and I can't stop myself from adding, "And if you're a good girl I'll bend you over one of those tombstones and fuck you until your soul leaves your body."

In answer her hand trails down the planes of my stomach until she reaches my cock. My traitorous cock that is hard and ready for another round. Emma's pleased murmur is enough to have it twitching against my stomach before she wraps her hand around it giving it a firm stroke.

I'm ready to roll over and show her the consequences of teasing me when she pushes on my chest as she sits up. I watch with wide eyes as she slides down the bed until she lays between my spread thighs. Her pale cheeks flush as she looks first at my cock and then at my face before licking the head.

"Emma-" I start to say.

I don't know what I was going to say next. One minute I'm talking and the next my mouth is hanging open while she does her damned best to suck my soul out of my body through the tip of my cock.

My hands grab the sheets on either side of my hips as she goes back down for another drag, her throat swallowing as she looks at me with large green eyes dark with desire. I see the devilish spark enter her eyes and I decide then and there that I'm going to fuck that pretty little mouth.

Her eyes get wider when my hands abandon their grip on the sheets to wind their way into her blonde hair. I give a slight tug to gauge her reaction, and the warm hum of her approval is all the permission I need. With dark lusty eyes she watches me as I guide her head up and down on my cock.

Her pink lips stretch so perfectly around my girth, the tiny freckle on her bottom lip nearly invisible as I drag her down my length.

Her hair tangles around my fingers so tightly they become white as I set a brutal pace. The wet sound of her mouth sucking my hard flesh has the darkness within me coming to life with a roar.

I come in her mouth with no warning, her eyes widen in surprise as she struggles to swallow every drop of my seed.

Releasing my hold on her hair I slump down on the bed. All the muscles that clenched when I came begin to relax, the warm soothing rush making me feel like I've just finished an intense workout at the gym.

Emma doesn't immediately join me. I watch with half lidded eyes as she wipes a bit of drool from her chin and then with a deviant glint in her green irises she latches onto my cock. Oversensitive from my orgasm my hips arch off the bed when she drags her tongue over the head of my cock. Each lick is its own torture as she watches me from underneath her lashes as she cleans my cock. Just when I don't think I can take anymore she releases me with an audible pop.

"Good boy." She purrs with a pleased smirk.

Can't have that.

"Come here." I say holding my arms out for her to come cuddle me.

She crawls up the bed until her head can rest solidly on my chest, but I don't give her the chance to relax. Grabbing her arm, I use her momentum to have her sprawl helplessly across my lap as I sit up.

"Thanks for the reminder, Babe." I say with a smile, "Being called a good boy reminded me what a *bad girl* you've been."

"Oh, no." She cries mockingly.

From this angle she can't see the smirk tugging at my lips. If she could, she might be a bit more serious. This isn't a funishment. It is a punishment, and by the end she's going to have a proper respect for me.

Ten solid strokes later and her tone is sincere once again.

"Who do you belong to?" I ask, using my grip on her hair to force her to look at me.

"You." She says her pools of emerald green watering with the aftermath of her spanking.

I help her sit up, her thighs landing on either side of mine. I wipe the tears away from her cheeks, wondering for a moment if I went too far. If I overplayed my hand and this is the moment where any hope for our future crashed and burned.

But then her smile returns, soft lips reddened from our earlier kisses stretching her mouth wide as she looks at me. Her hands land on my bare chest again and I shouldn't be surprised when she grinds herself against me. I noticed she was getting wet while I spanked her. The punishment for acting like a brat and trying to make me jealous made her ass red and I'm sure the pain will linger.

She coats my cock with her arousal as she grinds. God help me but her actions have me hardening underneath her. We need a break-to hydrate if nothing else. But as her movements continue, I find myself unable to stop her. Worse. I encourage it.

"Look at how needy you become in my bed." I say as I palm her breasts, "How desperately you need me to help you come."

I play with the soft flesh, kneading it gently as her breathing picks up. My tattoos seem bolder against her unmarked skin, the dark lines a stark contrast to the pale pink of her breasts.

As her head tips back, I take the opportunity to shift my hands from her breasts to her hips. Lifting her up I latch onto her nipple, tugging the sweet bud into my mouth. Rolling it against my tongue I listen to her pleas and cries as I distract her from where I've lined myself up with her dripping pussy. Releasing her nipple, I let go of her hips and let her sit down on my lap once more. Her eyes open just in time to see me spear her with my cock.

"Good thing I love a needy cunt." I say before guiding her hips up and down, using her body to work my length.

Her gasp at my words turns into a moan as I set a slow pace, letting the heat build for both of us. With multiple orgasms neither of us is desperate to come. Not yet. This one will be slow and gentle.

"Andrew." She says my name softly like a prayer as she rides me. "I don't think I can."

"You didn't think that when you were teasing my cock with your dripping pussy." I say with a dark tone, "You'll come on my cock like a good girlfriend, won't you?"

The words spark something dark in her eyes. A possessive streak that matches my own. My girlfriend. *Mine.*

Unable to help myself as possession rolls through my veins, I drive my hips up to meet hers. Her moans turn to screams as I hold her above me, hammering into her pussy from below.

Her muscles clamp down on me as her orgasm drenches my cock. Those muscles squeezing my length and milking me for every drop of seed I have left as I come inside her pretty pink pussy with a roar.

Emma and I lay in a pile of limbs napping for a

good chunk of the morning before I pull her into the shower in the late afternoon. If she's surprised that we shower together she doesn't comment. I wash and condition her hair, scratching her scalp softly with my nails as her eyes drift closed in contentment.

"We'll get lunch in town." I say while we dress.

While she rescheduled her flight for Sunday rather than tonight, I went out to the rental car and grabbed her luggage. Despite planning a shorter trip, her bag is stuffed with clothing, more than she would need for the weekend even. Emma hums her agreement for my lunch plan as she pulls on a black ruffled skirt that hits mid-thigh. It pairs well with her cream sweater.

"Your legs will get cold." I warn her, "When it gets dark the temperature drops rapidly in the mountains."

She holds up a pair of orange and black striped tights in response. I don't think it will be enough to keep the chill away, they stop above her knee. Not that I will complain about the eyeful of creamy skin it leaves on display.

I reach into the darkest recess of my closet to pull out a pair of black slacks and a dark grey sweater. It's the outfit I've used in the past for job interviews, and it is the nicest thing I have to wear. Watching as Emma curls her hair into loose waves, I feel the need to step up my game.

All the men at the festival will be wearing jeans and flannel shirts but I've always stood out. Slim and toned where the mountain men are broad and buff with muscles born of working outside in all elements. It's always been a tad off putting constantly comparing myself to them.

I catch her green-eyed gaze in the bathroom mirror when I come in to brush my teeth. I almost miss the way her eyes skim down the length of my body her pale cheeks flushing before her eyes dart back up to meet mine in the reflection. Emma's warm look of appreciation soothes the jagged edges of my pride. She barely spared Dave a glance at the diner. As farfetched as I find the possibility, it might just be possible that she would prefer me to the beefcakes wandering around.

A long drive up the mountain and I finally have Emma in Crescent Ridge. I see the way her eyes light up when she sees Main Street with its twin lines of shops. When it snows it looks like something straight out of a Hallmark movie and suddenly, I feel a dull ache in my chest when I think of Emma seeing that first snow in person.

"None of the businesses in my neighborhood bother decorating for Halloween." Emma tells me as we pass streetlights wrapped in orange and purple lights. Several full-size skeletons are posed on the sidewalk, some sitting on benches and others in more comical positions.

Emma laughs when we pass one that has its hand stuffed into an animatronic werewolf's mouth. With the festival in full swing, Main is packed with trucks, and we end up parking by Mrs. Carmichael's bakery, *Sugar Crossing*.

The plan was to pick up some sandwiches at the sub shop, but I can't deny Emma once she sees the window display. Cupcakes decorated with skulls, spiders, and broomsticks sit beside chocolate chip cookies shaped like pumpkins and witch hats.

Streamers of skeletons holding hands hang from the window and once we step inside, I notice the ceiling is covered in a fake spider web. Several plastic spiders hang suspended just above my head and Emma giggles when I run face first into one that I didn't see hanging lower.

"Andrew!" Mrs. Carmichael greets from behind her clear glass display counter, "It's been an age, if it's been a day! And who is this lovely woman? Finally send off for a bride of your own?"

I barely manage to fight my way out of the tangle of spider web while Emma introduces herself to the baker.

"Emma, pleased to meet you. I'm Andrew's girlfriend and I'm not a mail order bride. I love your shop!" She says in her bubbly manner.

"This is Mrs. Carmichael." I say stepping forward to finish introductions, "She's a local legend and can bake better than anyone you've seen on TV."

"Oh stop!" Mrs. Carmichael says waving a wrinkled hand to fight off my praise, "I just love baking and the boys love sweets."

The boys she refers to are fully grown lumberjacks who stand larger than the trees they cut down. Three sons who tower over their mother and can eat their way through a couple dozen cupcakes each.

Small with a grey bun, Mrs. Carmichael bustles around packing and ringing up our order. A chocolate chip witch hat for me and a skull cupcake for Emma. I wave her away when she offers to pay. She's spending the weekend in my town when she didn't plan to, and I'll be damned if the impulsive decision costs her a single dime.

"Face painting!" Emma shouts when she sees the advertisement in the window of the barbershop, "We *have* to get our faces painted."

I follow along as she leads me through the town. By the time we reach the hayride that will take us down to the festival proper she's met everyone. Thanks to the barbershop my face looks like a skull, fitting with my dark color scheme, and Emma has spider webs in purple and black that start at the crown of her head and arch down to her cheeks.

We've eaten our sweet treats and downed matching cups of warm apple cider, the sugar hitting Emma's bloodstream and causing her to vibrate on the haybale beside me.

Her hand wrapped in mine, the roses and thorns

sheltering her soft skin from the chilly evening air. Throughout our exploration of the town, she held my hand constantly and the few times we separated she stayed close never more than an arm length away.

In less than a day I've become accustomed to her casual touches. More than accustomed. Addicted.

The way she skips from booth to booth at the festival lights my heart. I'm dragged in her wake as she tugs me along, her excitement overflowing as her curls bounce along her back. She barely refrains from squealing when she spots the coffee tent.

Bean There is a lovely shop that I don't frequent often. In truth I prefer to keep to myself. I've interacted with more people today than in the last month, thanks in no small part to Emma. She does bring out the best in me.

Mama Mary flags us down after we have matching pumpkin spiced lattes in hand. A petite woman with short silver hair she's Daniel Hart's mother but for those of us without family on the ridge she's become a surrogate mother.

"Is this the Emma, I've heard so much about?" She asks before immediately pulling my girlfriend into a hug without waiting for an answer.

"Yes." I reply, "Emma this is Mama Mary. She's a bit of a mother to most of us, hence the nickname."

Emma watches fondly as Mary grabs me in a

tight hold. She pinches my cheek before letting us continue on our way with a promise to visit her soon.

Emma

I'm drunk on sugar, caffeine, and Andrew's intoxicating presence as I lead him through the festival grounds. A half dozen times I consider apologizing but each time I stop and begin to regulate my excitement I see his smile and bite back my words. Unlike so many others his patience doesn't wear thin under my unwavering barrage of enthusiasm.

"There is a maze." Andrew says leaning down to speak into my ear unbothered by the loud crowd of people mingling around us as we sip our lattes.

"Haunted?" I ask a bit breathlessly.

"Yes, but will a corn maze be enough?" He whispers back.

Judging by the dark look in his blue eyes he can read the thrum of desire burning in my veins. The thrill of the scare and the impending chase. The fear of not being able to find the exit as panic whips into a frenzy.

"Perfect." I say with a bright smile no doubt a bit heavy on the teeth.

Without another word he directs me through the

pedestrian traffic, finding a trash can for our cups on the way as he cuts a path through the stream of people. Every man we pass is draped in flannel and looks to be cut from the mountain we're standing on.

The girls back home would be too busy drooling over the mass of muscles walking around to notice the scent of roasted corn mingling with the cinnamon and nutmeg wafting over from the coffee tent. They would completely miss the slender man with tattoos, dark hair, and freckles I can't stop touching.

It's a miracle he hasn't complained about how I'm clinging to him like a barnacle on a ship's hull.

We wait in a long line for our turn in the maze every few minutes shuffling forward a few steps as people chatter around us. Several children run amok, most in their Halloween costumes. A bumblebee chases a witch with a bright green face. A ninja throws a corndog at a princess calling her snooty. Their laughter is high pitched carrying over the other sounds and I find myself entranced watching them run about.

"Do you want children?" Andrew's deep baritone takes me by surprise.

His chest is warm against my back, his arms wrapped loosely around my waist as he rests his chin on top of my head.

"Eventually." I answer, "You?"

"Impartial." He says just loud enough for me to hear, "But willing."

"I've always wanted three." I reply, "I have an older brother, but I always wanted a sister."

"Only child, but I would have liked having a sibling or two to share my childhood." He replies as we step forward, "I have divorced parents, who like to pretend the other doesn't exist. My presence makes that exceedingly difficult, so we speak twice a year and occasionally meet up for dinner when the guilt gets to them."

"I'm sorry." I whisper, squeezing his wrist with a gentle pressure that I hope is soothing.

"Don't be." He answers, "They were worse together. I will take apathy over fury any day. And their mistakes helped me learn what makes a relationship work. What makes it last through the trials and tribulations of life."

"Care to share your grand epiphany?" I ask.

"Three things closely entwined." He whispers into my ear, his warm breath sending chills down my arms.

"Passion." He says as he places a chaste kiss on my neck.

I should be shying away from his public display, but I can't bring myself to. Other couples are kissing and cuddling around us. Our little display is pure by comparison. It's the entirely impure memory of this morning that has me rubbing my thighs together discreetly.

"Obsession." His tattooed hand leaves my waist and wraps loosely around my throat.

The way his thumb strokes the long column of my neck has me trembling in Andrew's embrace. The way we cling to one another in bed and the way we click together like two long lost puzzle pieces always meant to join. It steals my breath from my lungs.

"Love." His voice is barely audible.

My heart stops dead in my chest at the word. A word so heavy and bold I can't breathe. I know he's not declaring his love for me. It's too soon. Logic wars with emotion as I inexplicably long for it to be more than a word.

I want his passion and obsession. I want his love.

No matter how short the timeframe it doesn't stop the pang of longing that fills my chest with my next breath.

"Loyalty." I say adding a fourth as I squeeze the hand still wrapped around my waist as I lean back into his hold.

His murmur of agreement stirs the fine hairs around my ear. We move forward with the line in silence, the weight of our words hanging heavy in the air.

When it's our turn the scarecrow running the maze hands us glow sticks. The faint screams of other entrants hit our ears, and I can't stop myself from grinning. Andrew follows behind me as I lead us into the maze.

The corn is a head taller than Andrew, the stalks planted so closely together that they form a wall on either side of us as we follow the path. A breeze blows through allowing the stalks to wave slightly in the wind, the leaves rustling as they brush against each other.

As the breeze stops, the rustling doesn't. My ears strain for any hint of sound as we come across the first split in the path marked by a jack o' lantern. Andrew's fingers trail down the back of my arm and I toss a grin over my shoulder at him.

Just as I'm about to ask left or right I see a large shadow move behind Andrew.

"Run!" I shout.

The grim reaper who bursts out of the wall of corn swipes at us with their scythe as we dart away laughing. Our feet slam into the soil the sound loud even to my own ears. We pause at the next intersection, our breathing coming out in heavy gasps.

Without hesitation Andrew reaches out and takes my hand pulling me down the path on the right. I fall into step beside him. A far off scream causes me to flinch drawing a laugh from Andrew.

His blue eyes are bright glowing in the dim light from the full moon as he steers us along the path.

I've never felt safer and simultaneously more on edge in my life.

Twice more we turn right and finally we reach a dead end. Doubling back the rumbling sound of a chainsaw sends my stomach churning as we run away without looking back.

"Is it just me or is this maze bigger on the inside?" I joke.

Glancing at my watch I see we've been in the maze for almost twenty minutes, and I can't hear the festival anymore. I know we're still on the correct path. It's lined with solar lights to keep us from tripping in the dark.

"Did you see the exit when we were in line?" Andrew asks.

I think back and although we saw dozens of people enter, I can't remember seeing any leave.

"No." I say quietly.

We walk in silence, hands still clasped between us as we wordlessly make our way back to the jack o' lantern. On this side of the path, I notice an orange sign staked in the ground with black lettering.

Feel like you've been here before?

I point out the sign to Andrew and we share a laugh. Taking the other path Andrew leads us down another fork choosing to go left. As I'm about to ask if he can hear anything a clown mask pops out of the corn beside me, and I scream.

Andrew pulls me away as my scream turns into a giggle.

"Fucking clowns." He mutters when we're far enough away the scare actor can't hear us.

"Not a fan?" I ask in a teasing tone.

I'm already wondering if I can get him to wear some face paint and chase me through the woods. Less birthday party or rodeo clown and more dark jester.

"Not a chance." Andrew says without looking at me, "Don't even think about it."

"Too late." I reply smiling cheekily.

His huff of laughter reaches my ears as we follow a curve in the path. The next fork has an altar set up with battery operated candles with plastic flames and jars of herbs sitting on a blood-stained tattered cloth. A sign sits in the middle of the table with two hands pointing in different directions.

Left or Right?

Live or Die?

"Do we go left?" I ask, "And choose life? Or is the sign just there to throw us off?"

"We might not even be close to the end." Andrew replies.

"Let's go." I say choosing the right path.

Andrew follows gamely as we amble forward. We reach another dead end with dozens of plastic tombstones and signs decrying our impending doom. We turn to retrace our steps, and a little girl steps out of the corn wearing a blue dress with ruffles and her blonde hair in pigtails. She squeezes a brown teddy bear to her chest as she twirls in front of us.

"You shouldn't be here." She says in a sing song voice, "The ghosts don't like the living."

She comes to a stop in front of us allowing us to see the heavy shadows painted beneath her eyes and the grey color of her skin. As she talks, I notice the line of fake blood painted on her neck.

"Only the dead linger here." A voice says behind us.

Andrew and I turn simultaneously to see the looming figure of a skeleton standing behind us.

"Run!" The little girl yells before releasing a high-pitched giggle.

We run without stopping back to the altar and hit the other path at a jog. We turn a corner, and the bright lights of the festival cause me to squint as we exit the maze.

Andrew spots a photographer set up nearby and walks us over. Dried corn and maize hangs from a pergola and the laminated backdrop has *Crescent Ridge 18th Annual Fall Festival* printed in bold black letters over some cartoon pumpkins.

"Proof we survived the maze." Andrew whispers in my ear while the photographer directs us into a pose underneath the pergola. "And documentation of our first official date."

He stands behind me with his arms wrapped around my torso as we pose for the photo. The warm puff of his breath on my chilled skin has me fighting back a shiver as I smile for the camera.

Andrew

"I was promised a graveyard." Emma's tone is teasing as I lead her back to my truck.

"Don't worry, I always keep my promises." I tell her as I hold open her door and offer her a hand up into the cab.

Her eyebrow flies up to her hairline, her face skeptical.

"It's a short drive." I promise before shutting her door.

Emma keeps up a constant chatter as I drive. She talks about the locals and their overly nosy questions.

"I swear I was asked no less than five times if I was a mail order bride." She says as the truck climbs a particularly steep hill.

"Women don't move out here for the scenery." I reply, "It's a small town and we're not exactly a tourist destination."

I can share her disbelief over the constant supply of brides choosing to marry the men of Crescent Ridge. I didn't think mail order brides were even a thing anymore before I moved out here. But they are and most of the couples I've met found each other through a mail order bride program. Some describe it as a dating app but for marriage.

Last week I couldn't imagine marrying a woman without dating her first. Now as I watch Emma talk animatedly with her hands waving as she illustrates her points, I don't find the idea so outrageous. If Emma signed up for the program, I would bend over backwards to convince her to pick me as her husband. Maybe the mountain men of Crescent Ridge have the right idea.

I pull into the gravel parking lot just outside the cemetery gates. The cemetery itself is on a hill with hundreds of graves dotting the site. All the graves are centuries old, with anyone who has died in the last century buried in Bramble's cemetery at the base of the mountain. This is no longer a location of grieving but rather a historical site that genealogists visit from time to time.

Turning off the truck, we're in complete darkness as we exit. With only the light of the moon, we make our way to the gate. Although it's closed there isn't a lock or a groundskeeper to prevent us from entering.

"Going to throw me a bone, Andrew?" She teases as we walk up the winding path that leads into the cemetery.

"Does the idea of a bunch of ghosts watching me fuck you get you wet?" I whisper into her ear. The autumn air has a chill to it, but I know the goosebumps running down her arms are from my breath on her heated skin.

"Maybe it's just the thought of getting railed on a tombstone under a full moon."

"Liar." I say leaning close enough to have my lips brush the shell of her ear, "You like the idea of showing them how well this hot little pussy takes my cock. How wet you get every time I fuck you like a good little slut. You're gonna come on that stone and let it drip down so they get a taste of what it's like to feel alive."

I don't comment on the audible hitch in her breath my words trigger. Guiding her off the stone path we walk across the grass passing statues of angels and busts made to resemble the dearly departed.

"Where do you want me?" She asks surveying the assortment of graves surrounding us.

I don't know if it's the late hour or the location that's got chills running down my spine, but my cock is hard as Emma prances in front of me. Her skirt lifts briefly as a breeze blows through blessing me with a glimpse of her bare ass. The wink she shoots over her shoulder tells me everything I need to know.

I don't deign to respond to her question. I grab her wrist tugging her over to a sunken mausoleum. Leading her down the stone steps I swing open the heavy door brushing aside the cobwebs hanging down as I drag her to the center of the crypt.

Caskets line the walls with brass plates listing the names and birth and death dates. Emma gasps as she looks around the room, but she doesn't look frightened. Her eyes shine with an eagerness I should have expected.

"Here?" Emma asks with the slightest tremble in her voice.

If I didn't know her, I would attribute it to fear rather than excitement. Pressing close I slip a hand underneath her skirt, my fingers finding her bare pussy with ease.

"You're fucking soaked, Emma." I growl as I lean her back on the stone slab sitting in the middle of the room.

"Fuck me, Andrew." She pleads as her knees fall open putting her wet pussy on display.

The pale pink lips are shiny with arousal even with the little light making its way to us. Just the sight of her spread out like a feast ready for the taking is twisting my stomach into knots. Despite her urgency I don't give in to her demands. She's not the one in control and she needs a reminder.

I slap her clit with a light tap of my fingers. Her resulting yelp brings a smirk to my face.

"You're in no position to give orders." I say as I stroke a finger over her clit.

Seeing her shiver underneath my touch elicits a possessive urge to pin her down and pound my cock into her until she comes screaming my name.

"Please." She pleads as I rub stiff fingers through her wet folds.

She tries to wiggle her hips in a bid to get closer, to fuck herself on my fingers, but I put a quick stop to that. With a firm hand I press her hips down hindering her movements and causing her to groan.

"Listen to you." I say as I thrust my fingers into her sharply pulling yet another moan from her lips, "Moaning and groaning like a ghost. If anyone wanders by this graveyard tonight, they'll think this place is truly haunted."

With her head tossed back as she strains against my restricting hand in vain, I doubt she's following the flow of my words. Seeing her eyes squeezed shut tempts me to slap her clit again, but I don't want to pull my fingers out of her pussy.

"Emma." I purr as I lean over her.

My fingers go still just shy of her G-spot.

"A-Andrew." She moans in supplication.

"Emma." I say, "Let me see those pretty green eyes."

Her lashes part and I get the tiniest glimpse of emerald before I curl my fingers brushing her G-spot and she closes her eyes again.

"Emma." I murmur in admonishment.

This time her eyes open wider, the brilliant green flashing with annoyance that I've stopped my exploration again.

"Andrew." She chides, "If you don't-"

My fingers slip out before she finishes saying my name. The second slap to her clit cuts off her sentence abruptly.

"You're not in charge, Babe." I tell her letting my smugness color my tone.

She lies beneath me compliant as I return my fingers to her pussy. Her eyes fixate on me, the pupils blown wide nearly swallowing the green rings as I pump my fingers. I can't look away from her eyes as she begins to breathe in heavy gasps that match the pace of my fingers.

Wet squelching sounds echo around the stones surrounding us as Emma's muscles begin to flutter and pulse around my fingers. The obscene sounds go straight to my cock making my blood rush south as it goes impossibly harder. I can feel the zipper carving a pattern into the hard flesh.

"Soak this stone." I command as she clamps down, "Give these ghosts a taste of your juicy pussy."

Her body goes tight like it's seizing her arms and legs flexing as she comes around my fingers. The muscles squeezing me milk my fingers in a shallow imitation of what will happen when she comes again on my cock.

Inaudible grumbling meets my ears when I withdraw my fingers. Sucking the pair into my mouth I close my eyes when the taste of Emma bursts on my tongue.

"Eyes on me, Babe." Emma says nudging my hip with her bent knee.

She lies before me, body slack and satisfied but there is a dark hunger in her eyes begging for more. Begging for every inch of my cock and every drop of pleasure I can wring from her body.

I let her teasing command slide, ignoring her mocking tone as I unbuckle my belt, tapping the metal frame against the inside of her thigh. She shies away from the cold touch of steel as I finish freeing my cock from the harsh confines of my pants. Rising onto her elbows she eyes me with a blatant hunger that causes my chest to swell with male pride.

None of those mountain men could handle this woman. They might have stacks of muscles but not a single damn one of them would match her level of kink. None of them would bring her to orgasm in a graveyard surrounded by skeletons and restless spirits.

A chill wind blows through the open door carrying the short howls of a pack of coyotes. Emma freezes underneath me, her expression morphing from arousal to fear as she reaches out to grasp my forearms. Her nails bite into my skin as I smile down at my girlfriend.

"Not afraid of ghosts haunting us for desecrating

their sacred resting place but a pack of coyotes has you running scared?" I say as I rub the head of my cock through her slick lips.

"One is a far more pressing danger." She scolds even as I see the spark of desire reignite in her green eyes.

A single thrust has me sliding into the hilt the low timber of my moan overshadowing her breathy gasp.

"The door is open." Emma protests even as she clutches me closer as I begin to move my hips, "They can come in."

I let her panic build for a moment, the fear adding to her arousal as I thrum her clit with my thumb in time with my thrusts.

"They're not close by." I reassure her.

My hands push her thighs to the side splaying her open to allow my cock to sink deeper.

"You can't know that." She argues.

Emma is close to the edge again, her breath coming in short fast puffs that are visible in the chilly air.

"Too weak." I mutter between thrusts, doing my best to stave off my own orgasm, "They're miles away."

Her eyes are wide open watching the door over my shoulder and the irritation that she doesn't trust me to protect her at her most vulnerable causes me to pinch her clit in reproach.

"I'm the only creature you need to be worried about

right now." I say when her eyes dart back to my face.

Without missing a beat, I reach out and wrap my hand around her throat. The black ink of my tattoos looks beautiful against her flushed skin. Squeezing gently, I see the exact moment she forgets about the coyotes. They're still howling, the sounds slowly growing quieter as they move further away.

"A pretty girl like you doesn't need to worry about anything other than gripping my cock tight and coming like you're told." I say.

Unable to argue with my hand around her throat she melts under the force of my thrusts as I drive her closer to the edge. I don't let up with her compliance. Emma's fingers turn white as they grip my forearms, her eyes liquid pools of desire as she comes on my cock.

I continue thrusting through her orgasm until I can't ignore the tight grip of her warmth anymore and I come with a loud moan. Emma's hands comb through my hair as I lay slumped against her chest. The steady rise and fall of her chest with every breath soothing me as she strokes her hands down my neck and begins kneading my shoulders.

A breeze causes us both to shiver and I pull back with reluctance. Maybe we'll repeat this little act on a warm summer night but right now I need to get Emma into the truck so she can warm up before she catches a cold. Pulling off my sweater I stuff it over her head without acknowledging her protests.

"You'll get cold." She murmurs even as she sticks her arms through the sleeves.

She swims in folds of fabric, the hem falling lower than her skirt as she stands up on wobbly legs. Her curls are destroyed, leaving her with a frizzy blonde halo and I can't hide my dopey smile.

"What?" She asks when she notices me staring, "Do I have coffee breath?"

She begins to ramble. Of course, we both have coffee breath, but I don't see how that could be an issue. I like the taste of pumpkin spice on her tongue. Leaning over I kiss her until she melts against me, all worries and concerns gone with the wind.

Her fingers go to my belt buckle, and I swat her away with a laugh.

"Home." I scold her as I grab her hand and begin leading her back to the truck, "It's getting too cold for another round. The ghosts will just have to be satisfied with the show they got."

Emma

One long weekend with the man of my dreams and reality comes crashing down Sunday morning. I'm expected back at work on Monday and that means I have a flight to catch. No more mind-blowing sex or cuddles in my immediate future.

"I wish I didn't have to leave." I tell him, "My job and my friends would lose their minds if I didn't go back home though. I didn't tell them I was meeting anyone this weekend."

His blue eyes flick to mine angrily from where he is unloading the dishwasher. Aside from another trip to the diner and the festival foods we scarfed down, Andrew has made all our meals, and for a man living alone on a mountain he is a fantastic cook.

"Are you serious?" He snaps.

For a moment I think he's outraged that I kept him a secret.

"You came to meet a random man without telling anyone? What if I were a serial killer?" He adds before I can reply.

His hands are in his hair and he's pacing the length of his kitchen barefoot while I stand in the doorway watching him.

"You're not." I mumble.

"You didn't know that three days ago!" He shouts, raising his hands above his head as if to direct an airplane onto a runway.

"Congrats!" I say sarcastically, "Now you sound like a psycho."

"Good!" He says matching my tone, "I need to be one to look after you."

"I don't need you to look after me." I snarl.

As if I need a fucking keeper. I'm a full-grown woman and I don't need a man to take care of me. I got enough of that treatment from my parents and my brother. I don't need it from Andrew too.

"Your pussy says otherwise." He replies with a smug look as if the argument is settled.

His words shock me into silence long enough for him to grab a duffel bag out of his closet. I watch as he begins folding shirts and jeans before stuffing them in the bag.

"Where are you going?" I ask a little miffed that he's that eager to get away from me that he can't wait for me to leave for the airport.

"Atlanta, apparently." He mutters as he adds socks and underwear to the bag.

"Seriously?" I ask even as I grab his cell phone charger and laptop from beside the bed and hand them to him.

"Yes. I'm not letting a sexual deviant like you roam freely in a city full of innocent unsuspecting people." His tone is serious but the slight smirk curling his lips says otherwise.

"I didn't invite you." I say crossing my arms and trying to act nonchalant when inside I'm a puddle of goo.

This isn't the end. We're not parting ways to inevitably end up in a frustrating long-distance relationship held together by willpower and video chats.

"Your mouth didn't but something else sure did." He says before his eyes drop to where the zipper of my jeans hides me from his gaze.

"Stop that!" I scold.

His answering laugh makes my heart skip a beat as I try not to blush. The deep rumbly baritone never fails to send my heart racing. Not to mention its effect on *other* areas of my body.

"Hurry up or we're going to miss our flight." Andrew says as he walks by to get something from his closet.

His hand smacks my ass on the way and despite the thick fabric of my skirt my ass is still stinging when he returns with a pair of over the ear headphones clasped in his hands. The smirk is a permanent fixture at this point and while I'd love to wipe it from his face a quick glance at the clock proves his point.

We don't have time to waste.

"You don't have a ticket." I mutter wondering if I can reschedule my flight again.

Surely the travel insurance will cover a last-minute cancellation. Instead of flying out this morning we can leave tonight. And it will give Andrew more time to pack to ensure he doesn't forget anything.

"Bought one yesterday." Andrew says as he hands me his phone to show me his ticket information.

For all the sudden argument and packing this isn't a last-minute decision on his part. He wanted it to be a surprise. His stuffed duffel bag lands next to my sticker slapped suitcase and he looks at me expectantly.

Waiting for me to agree. To invite him. I know without a doubt if I said no, he wouldn't follow me. Andrew is without a doubt a good man and a gentleman. Both rare qualities on their own never mind the statistics of finding both in a single man.

"Let's go." I say trying for a tone of exasperation but judging by the broad smile on Andrew's face my excitement is obvious.

I can't hide my feelings from this man. He sees right through my layers to the darkest hidden corners of my soul with ease. As he grabs our luggage before walking me out to my rental car, I can admit at least to myself that I don't want to hide them anymore. Not from Andrew.

There's something building between us. Something I'm scared to name but desperate to explore, and I think Andrew feels it too.

Andrew

Catching our flight out of Bramble is easy. The airport is tiny with only a few flights leaving each day. A few years ago, we would have had to fly out in a puddle jumper rather than a 747. Ignoring the call for first class boarding I sit with Emma until her group is called. She was quiet the entire ride over and I can see the nervous pulse fluttering in her neck every few minutes.

She's nervous. Maybe about the flight but more likely she's having second thoughts about our relationship and how quickly it's progressing. I'm no fool. I know that I'm speeding things along at a reckless pace, but I can't help it. If I don't give this everything I have, then I know I'll regret it for the rest of my life.

A woman like Emma is a once in a lifetime kind of find. Everything about us clicks together so seamlessly, so perfectly. Even the odd parts.

"Nice." Emma says as I plop down into the seat beside her.

The man who I exchanged seats with ambles away with the first class ticket I purchased clutched between his fingers with a gleeful expression. I didn't want to rely on a random stranger's kindness, so I bought a better seat hoping to entice Emma's seatmate with an upgrade and it worked.

"I wasn't going to let my girlfriend sit by herself." I say nonchalantly.

Emma's hand grabs mine with an unexpected fierceness. Her nails cut into the soft flesh of my palm like tent stakes driving into dirt.

"I can't decide if that makes you chivalrous or possessive." She whispers mindful of the people seated around us.

"Both." I whisper back.

Her delighted giggle is enough to have me grinning like a lovesick dope during takeoff. She clings to me the entire time wrapped around my arm like she's afraid I'll vanish if she lets go.

Once we're in the air and all the other passengers are preoccupied with their books or the in-flight movie I lean over to whisper in Emma's ear.

"I have a fantasy I'd like you to consider."

She doesn't respond verbally but I see the way she bites her bottom lip to keep from smiling and the way her green eyes glint with desire.

"Ever fancy joining the mile high club?" I ask letting my lips graze her ear as I whisper the words.

"I'm game." She whispers back and after some furtive glances to ensure the coast is clear I lead the way to the bathroom.

Ridiculously tiny, there is barely enough room for us both to stand with the door closed. I nearly suggest ditching the entire idea but then Emma brushes against me and all the blood rushes from my brain to my cock.

"You are going to need to be quiet." I whisper as Emma sits on the sink.

"You're the one with the filthy mouth." She retorts.

"I was referring to the way you moan every time I fuck you." I say as I unbuckle my belt.

"I do not-" She begins to argue, her voice rising without her notice, and I lunge forward to silence her.

Our kiss isn't sweet or gentle. Emma matches my aggression with equal fervor, her teeth biting at my bottom lip and her tongue darting forward to tangle with mine. She doesn't let me move an inch as she attacks my mouth barely giving me enough space to free my cock and flip up her skirt.

I thrust, her pussy slick and hot as she takes every inch. I swallow her moans even as I grab her hips and hold her in place as I begin fucking her. We don't have time to linger if we don't want to get caught.

She clutches my shoulders through my shirt, the nails biting into my skin despite the thin cotton barrier. I'm helpless to do anything more than drive my hips into hers seeking relief for the heat climbing up my spine as she clings to me.

When our mouths part and I suck in a deep breath of air, Emma lets out a moan. I slap a hand over her mouth, but I worry the damage is done. The sounds of our bodies meeting are loud enough in the tiny room. Emma's green eyes flare bright as she continues to moan against my palm. With my hand clasped tightly over her mouth she's free to make as many sounds as she wants.

I'm the one who has to keep their mouth shut to avoid discovery and it's harder than I expected not to tell Emma exactly what she's doing to me. How her body bends eagerly to my will and how much I like the way she moans every time she takes my cock.

Her teeth bite down on the flesh of my palm when she comes, her scream muffled. Her muscles clamping down on my cock drags my orgasm from the steady build of warmth to a blazing inferno of heat in seconds. Helpless to prolong our pleasure, I come in Emma with a loud moan closing my eyes and throwing my head back.

When I open my eyes, Emma is looking at me with a mixture of contentment and trepidation.

Shit.

Righting our clothes takes a moment and some careful maneuvering. No matter how I try to smooth down my hair it springs back up in willful clumps. Emma is no better, her cheeks are still flushed and there is a clear red imprint from where my hand was over her mouth. Only an idiot wouldn't know what we've been up to. At least the marks on Emma's face will fade in a few minutes.

A loud knock on the door makes us both freeze, looking at each other with wide eyes.

"It's going to be a while." I call out, "Flying never agrees with me!"

Emma's hands fly up to cover her mouth as she struggles to muffle her giggles. The masculine sigh on the other side of the door precedes a grumble before we hear the man walk away. Our eyes meet knowingly. If we can hear his footsteps there is no telling what anyone walking by could hear.

"I'll go first." I tell Emma, "Wait five minutes and follow."

I want to gauge the situation and do what I can to mitigate any embarrassment before she leaves the bathroom.

I press one last chaste kiss to her lips before I slip out the door. Walking back to our seats nothing seems out of place. Everyone is still dialed into their choice of distraction. Just as I reach our seats, I hear Emma's soft footsteps behind me.

I don't address her disobedience with words. My eyebrow rises in reproach, but Emma doesn't look remorseful. She knows just as well as I do how it looks for us both to walk back together.

I meet the eye of an elderly woman, looking over at

us from across the aisle. Her cloudy brown eyes are hidden behind thick tortoise shell glasses, but her smile is knowing. She winks at me before turning back to her ereader.

"We need to work on your discretion." I murmur to Emma as I open the little bottle of water the attendant provided after takeoff.

She peers at me from beneath her lashes as she scans me with a keen eye.

"I'm not the one who couldn't help but moan like a whore when he came." Her soft-spoken words cause me to choke on my water.

"You're going to pay for that dirty mouth." I growl into her ear.

Relaxing back into my seat, I settle in to watch the comedy playing on the small screen attached to the back of the seat in front of me. Emma's head lands softly on my shoulder as she cuddles close to me, her eyes fixed on the same screen.

By the time the credits roll the attendants are directing us to fasten our seatbelts for landing. Emma's hands clutch my arm tightly while we taxi down the runway.

"I can't wait to get home." Emma says to me as we walk through the metropolitan airport in search of the baggage claim.

"Exhausted from roughing it in the mountains?" I tease knocking my shoulder against hers.

"Hardly roughing it." She replies with a giggle, "Your cabin is huge compared to my apartment. Just you wait and see."

As Emma watches for our luggage, I clear my throat. No time like the present to bring up something a little awkward.

"I was thinking I could stay in a hotel while I'm here." I say fixing my eyes on the spinning carousel loaded with bags, "I don't want to cramp your style."

"Don't be stupid." Emma says shortly, "Cramp my style? That phrase is older than my grandpa. You need to get out more."

Her words are reassuring but I can't help but feel that I'm pushing her into a situation that she might find uncomfortable.

"You weren't expecting to come home with a guest much less a boyfriend in tow and-" I begin to rationalize but she cuts me off.

"I stayed in your home. You'll stay in mine." She glares, daring me with her eyes to disagree with her again and I swallow the rest of my protest.

"Now be a darling and grab our bags." She says rocking back on her heels, "I'm still a little *exhausted* from the plane ride. I've got this tight spot in my lower back from sitting awkwardly."

I bite my bottom lip to stop myself from grinning as I lean over to grab her suitcase and my duffel.

"I'll rub it later." I tell her as she leads us out of the

airport.

The crowd of bodies surrounding us is overwhelming at first, but Emma doesn't seem bothered. I keep my eyes on her as she floats ahead of me making a direct line for a parking garage.

I nearly die when she leads me to her car. In a lot filled with sedans, vans, and trucks in neutral colors she has the only car wrapped in a bright red color with a character from *Legion X* sprawled across the hood.

"You nerd." I say between laughs.

"Shut it." She replies with a fierce scowl.

Riding in the passenger seat of her car is an experience. During the quick drive to her apartment, I had no shortage of fidgets and baubles to play with, which was a good thing considering how nerve wracking the trip was. The mini Rubik's cube I found in the center console saved my sanity. I was right to worry about Emma driving down the mountain. The woman could barely manage to drive from the airport to her apartment complex without getting into an accident.

No turn signals. Zero attention to blind spots. And an inhumane rage directed at her fellow drivers for simply existing. It would be a civil service to disconnect and hide her battery. The Atlanta PD might just give me a medal.

The complex is brick with a glass front door that

doesn't lock, and the entire lobby smells like mildew. I ignore the urge to wrinkle my nose, but the disgust must show on my face because she immediately adopts a sheepish expression.

"Cosplay is an expensive hobby, and this was the cheapest option that made sense." She says as she leads me over to a flight of stairs, "The neighborhood is decent and it's close to my work and downtown."

I don't comment on the elevator that has a faded out of order sign taped to it. Or the carpeted steps that are an unsettling shade of brown. Everywhere I look as we climb thirteen flights of steps is another reason not to live here. I hate cities. I went to college in Chicago and four years later I couldn't get far enough away from the crowds.

Emma's apartment number is 13b and her door is made of the same cheap particle board as the rest of her floor. She grumbles as she fights with the lock for a few moments, the latch sticking before she manages to shoulder it open. I could open her front door with a butter knife easier than with her key. The door creaks open and I make a note to pick up some WD-40 for the latch and the hinges. And a few other things to make her home more secure.

"Don't get the wrong idea." She tells me as she leads me into her apartment, "It's only this tidy because I wanted to come back to a clean home."

Her home is a reflection of her, bright and

warm with a distinct lavender scent that instantly makes me feel at home despite the unfamiliar surroundings. It's a two bedroom apartment, and her bedroom has a bed large enough for us to share with a black and white sheet set with a spiderweb pattern embroidered on the comforter buried underneath a dozen pillows in matching colors.

The entire apartment screams her love for the spooky holiday. Fake spiderwebs and tattered cloth drapes every available surface, and she has bloody decals scattered around her walls. Fake skulls decorate her coffee table, and she has several white pillar candles littered throughout the apartment.

The other bedroom is sparse with no other furniture than a desk buried under mounds of aluminum.

"Some are for me, and some are custom orders from people I meet at conventions." She tells me when I ask about the chain mail armor replicas.

"Nice little side hustle." I compliment.

"More like obsession." She says as she walks over to the closet door to reveal dozens of completed sets.

"Is that one from *Medieval Slayer*?" I ask pointing at a bright red set.

"Yes!" She answers with pride, "You play?"

We talk video games as she unpacks her suitcase and makes room for my clothes in her closet. She doesn't ask how long I'm staying and I'm grateful for that small mercy, because I don't have an answer.

A week. Maybe more if we continue to click like we have this past weekend. I can work from anywhere, and working from Emma's home with its navy blue walls and overabundance of soft pillows wouldn't be a chore.

Everywhere I look there is evidence of Emma. Mugs with nerdy quotes in the kitchen and framed movie posters hanging on the living room walls. I hate the city but I'm beginning to think I could love her enough to live anywhere.

Emma

"What do you want for dinner?" I ask from the pile of blankets I am currently bundled inside.

"I think a black hole swallowed the contents of your fridge." He replies from his seat on the couch sans blanket.

Too hot he complains, but he still lets me snuggle against his side.

"Obviously I meant takeout." I say poking a finger into his side, "Chinese, Mexican, or pizza?"

"Hm." He hums noncommittedly as he considers the options.

I have dozens of menus pinned to the fridge. He doesn't know it yet but he's not only going to fetch one but also place the order. I'll pay for it, but I am done peopling today. First the close confines of the plane and then the crowded airport were too much.

Andrew begins peeling back my blankets despite my grumbled protests. Once he has wiggled his way into my cocoon, he curls his long body around mine, the heat of his body too much in addition to the multiple layers.

"I *am* hungry." He whispers, blowing warm air

against my neck, "But not for food."

"Insatiable." I whisper back before his lips claim mine.

Compared to our rushed encounter on the plane this time we linger in every moment and every kiss. He kisses me like the world stands still around us. The wet hot press of his lips to mine has the tips of my fingers tingling with static. My hot core beats in time with my heart, the blood a dull roar in my ears with each pulse. Uncaring if I appear needy, I claw at his clothes like a woman possessed.

He doesn't laugh or tease me as I strip him of his clothes. A fond indulgent smile curves the corners of his lips up as he watches me with those bright blue eyes behind his glasses.

Minutes or hours pass as I explore the vast expanse of his chest and stomach. The faint line of dark hair that leads beneath the heavy denim waistband of his jeans finally drawing my attention. A noticeable bulge strains against the zipper but I'm in no rush. Not yet.

"You look a little warm." Andrew murmurs before I drag my nails lightly down his chest.

His resounding moan causes another pulse between my thighs. I could strip him of his pants and ride him to completion right now. My orgasm would come fast and easy, but I want to stretch this out.

Savor this man and his delectable body. Sear the

image of him arching into my touch into my very brain. I want to live in this moment forever.

Andrew helps me peel out of my clothes, the chilly apartment air doing nothing to dampen the heat building between us. The way our bodies slide against each other is a dance unlike any other.

"Open up for me." He says as he tilts me back on the couch, the pile of blankets underneath my back.

My thighs fall open leaving my pussy exposed as he rocks back onto his heels to stare at me.

"So pretty." He whispers more to himself than to me.

His thumbs part my folds, and I watch as he looks at my dripping center. His blue eyes darken with a fierce hunger as they fixate on my clit. The pad of his thumb rough against the sensitive flesh hidden by my folds. Beginning slowly, he circles my clit never touching it directly. Round and round he goes each pass winding my pleasure up another notch.

Those dark eyes never lose their focus. He is immune to my whimpers and my pleas. I come in a rush, liquid heat dripping from my core. No words of praise or filth greet my ears.

Andrew's pupils grow until the blue of his iris is barely visible. After my second orgasm he leans in and sucks my clit into his mouth without any warning. Barely a second of warm wet pressure on the bundle of nerves and I come with a scream clutching at the blankets beneath me. I try to speak but all I hear is incoherent babbling.

Three orgasms and I am done. I can't take anymore.

I pull and yank on Andrew's dark hair until his mouth releases my clit with an audible pop. Convinced he is done, I release his hair and relax back against the couch. The first lick jolts me upright.

A harsh grip on my hips keeps my butt pinned to the couch, splayed open for his enjoyment. He's vocal again. His sounds and words of praise are muffled by the sensitive pink folds of my pussy. A delicate humming sound sends vibrations through my core and my entire body tenses as I come again.

"Please." I beg, "No more. I can't take another."

"Do you remember your safe word?" Andrew asks as he pulls away.

His mouth and chin are shiny with the evidence of my arousal, but his eyes are laser focused on my face. Looking for signs of discomfort, I realize. During our chats on SoulConnect's app we each chose a safe word. A word we could use at any time to immediately stop any sexual activity.

Mine is carrots, the one vegetable I've never liked, and Andrew chose pineapples. Same category he said when I asked his reasoning.

"Yes." I reply slightly breathless.

Andrew arches a dark brow as he looks at me and waits. We stare at each other for a beat of time and then another. It soon becomes clear he's going to sit there as motionless as a statue until I either use my safe word or give verbal consent.

"I don't need to use my safe word." I tell him directly, "I want to continue."

He doesn't reply verbally, just leans down to give me a sweet kiss that tastes like a mixture of the mint candy he ate on the plane and my own musk. Distracted by his mouth and very wicked tongue I gasp in shock when he pushes his cock inside me. The grin on his face when he pulls away is dark and devious.

Not waiting for me to adjust he moves quickly as he begins to drive his cock into me in a brutal rhythm. I'm helpless to do more than take it. My hands scrabble for purchase on his shoulders, my nails digging in as I slide up the couch. Andrew pulls me back, impaling me on his cock and I reach over my head to push against the arm of the couch. Holding myself in place I watch as Andrew grabs my ankles and lifts them over one shoulder.

The new angle allows him to slide impossibly deeper, each pump of his hips working the breath from my body.

"Such a lovely little girlfriend, taking my cock like you were made for it." Andrew growls above me.

I can't answer between gasps, but he doesn't need a response.

"Made to be fucked by me." He says a second later.

I let out some shrill sound that he takes as agreement.

"Yes." He groans, "Listen to that."

He closes his eyes and tilts his head back as he continues to pound into me. A look of bliss softens his expression as he listens to the wet slap of our bodies colliding.

The obscene sounds combine with the harsh grip of his fingers biting into the flesh of my hip to drive me higher. Unable to stop it, I come crying Andrew's name as my muscles squeeze and milk his cock.

"That's it Babe. Take every drop." He says hips pulsing as his seed coats my walls in warm spurts.

We lie in a boneless heap, the blankets beneath my back clinging to our sweaty skin as we catch our breath.

"Chinese." He says later.

It takes entirely too long for me to realize what he's talking about. Wordlessly I point at the fridge.

Sweet and sour chicken for me and cashew beef for him with a side of vegetable rolls to split. Andrew dutifully orders the food without complaint, amusement curling his lips when I make him answer the door. My refusal to put on clothes until the food arrives causes his eyes to darken with lust once more but he keeps his hands to himself until after dinner.

Over the next two weeks we fall into a comfortable routine. Each morning I wake up after Andrew to find him cooking breakfast before I leave for work, and he sets up his laptop in the living room.

After the first week I tidy up my incomplete projects and offer him the spare room as an office space for him to work in. After work I either cook dinner or we order takeout, and we watch TV together. Sometimes it's fantasy or sci-fi that we watch and other times it's trashy reality TV that my friends have me hooked on. And then we fuck like bunnies. No place in my tiny apartment is safe. We discover the kitchen table I got from Ikea that I always thought was flimsy is sturdy enough to bear my weight.

Andrew doesn't mention returning to Colorado and I'm too fucking scared to ask if he's staying. I want him to stay but every time I try to bring it up the words choke in my throat. And how crazy is that? It's barely been two weeks. It's too soon to ask a man to move in with me. Way too crazy.

But it feels like he's already moved in. He fixed my door the first day while I was at work. My key now turns easily in the lock, so I don't have to fight my door every day and the hinges no longer creak. Then he unclogged the shower drain without complaining about the excessive amount of hair he pulled out. Day by day he did little bits of maintenance to make my home more comfortable and not once did he call attention to it. And now I'm trying not to read too much into it. Trying not to assume it's an act of love.

Doesn't stop me from wanting to ask though. Doesn't stop me from wanting to tell him that I love him, and I never want him to leave. Doesn't stop the tension from melting out of my body each time I come home to find him wrapping up his work or folding a pile of laundry. His neat folds are precise in a manner my hands will never achieve.

It's insane. Completely.

"You did what?" Jill asks in a voice approaching shrill.

I look around and apologize to the tables near us with a sheepish expression. Even sitting outside on the patio of our favorite restaurant we can't be *that* loud. I joined my two friends for lunch. They were getting fussy that I cancelled on girl's night last week and I've missed them. And I haven't told them about Andrew yet. Hence Jill's tone.

"I met a man on a dating app-" I begin to reply, and she cuts me off with a dismissive wave.

"I heard you." Jill says her dark gaze pinning me in place before she swings her head to look at Gabriella, "Did you hear her? That she met a stranger online and didn't tell anyone that she was flying out to meet him?"

Gabriella tilts her head, her red ponytail following the movement as she looks at me appraisingly.

"I heard her." She tells Jill.

Jill's dark brown hair is pinned in a perfectly flawless bun, not a strand out of place.

"He could have been an axe murderer!" She whisper shouts mindful of the crowded patio.

"He's not." I argue, "He's sweet and he's a total weirdo but not in a bad way."

Jill stares at me, her eyes wide in disbelief. Gabriella sips her coffee as her gaze darts back and forth between us, gauging the level of tension.

"At least you came back safely." Jill mutters after a minute, "Can't believe you didn't let us vet him before you went out there to meet him."

Ignoring Jill's muttering Gabriella turns to me.

"It's been two weeks since you got back. Was the sex really that good that you're still hung up on this stranger you'll never see again?"

I clam up fast. Jill drops a chip back onto her plate as both women eye me with piercing looks.

"You'll never see him again, right?" Jill asks, "I mean he's in Colorado."

"Long distance?" Gabriella asks with a gleam in her eye.

Ever since she met Oliver, she's been more of romantic than ever before. You never know when you're going to meet your soulmate, she says all the time. Meeting her husband in a rideshare mix up right before Christmas, her favorite holiday, has her meddling in our love lives more than ever before.

"He's visiting." I say in a small voice.

"Visiting? Like for a weekend?" Gabriella asks, "Are you trying to do long distance then?"

It's Jill who sees the truth before I can say it. She's always been perceptive. Too perceptive.

"He came back with you." She says, "He's been here two weeks, and you haven't introduced us?"

"Is it true?" Gabriella squeals bouncing in her seat with excitement, "Can we meet him? Is he a ghoul head too?"

"Does he even have a job?" Jill cuts in over Gabriella's rambling.

"He works remotely." I tell them first to soften the protective rage simmering inside Jill.

"Does he pay rent?" Jill asks.

"We haven't talked about it-" I start to reply.

"That fucking bum!" She shouts and no longer caring about the people around us I find my temper rising.

"Stop it!" I shout back and she reels back in her seat no doubt shocked by my tone.

"He's not a bum. I haven't brought up bills because I haven't asked him how long he's staying. He buys groceries and orders takeout for both of us. He fixes all the little things around the apartment that I haven't been able to get maintenance to look at yet. The faucets. The drains. Hell, he even installed an additional lock on my door to make it safer." I rant until I feel blue in the face.

She's skeptical and I can understand why. It sounds outlandish and ridiculous from an outsider's perspective. But she hasn't met Andrew. She hasn't spent the last two weeks falling in love with the perfect man. Not that he would be perfect for Jill. She would murder him before her first Monday morning meeting. But for me, he is perfect.

"He likes Halloween." I add after a second.

Not as much as I do of course. My apartment is heavily decorated for the upcoming holiday, but his house didn't have a single pumpkin or fake cobweb to be found.

"We're meeting him." Jill says with a steely tone.

"He sounds like a keeper." Gabriella adds with a warm smile.

I don't mention that if I didn't want them to meet him, I wouldn't have brought him up. But he's quickly becoming an irreplaceable part of my life, and I want him to meet my friends. We make plans for the weekend, a nice dinner at my apartment so that I have time to prepare him for Jill's animosity and Gabriella's optimism.

There's no more dodging the subject now. We have to define our relationship before Jill launches an interrogation that would make the CIA nervous.

Andrew

"How long are you staying?" The petite brunette asks as she storms past me when I open the apartment door.

I could protest, but that would only drag this out. I know without asking that this fiery woman is Jill, and she is here to bust my balls. I'm about to close the door and answer her impertinent question when a second woman with red hair waltzes through the door.

"Nice to meet you, Andrew." Gabriella says as she brushes past me.

"Likewise." I mutter after glancing down the hallway to ensure that all my interrogators are present.

Emma's friends are easy to recognize from the photos littered around her apartment. Photos from conventions with Jill pinned to the fridge and a group photo with Jill, Gabriella, and her husband Oliver from last Christmas framed on the mantel.

"So?" Jill asks spinning on her heel in the living room to face me with a fierce glare.

She has her hip cocked and an impatient frown on

her face as she waits for my reply.

"As long as she'll let me." I answer.

"Oh my God!" Jill shouts, "You're sleeping with her so you can stay here!"

Her eyes are wide and she's pointing her finger at me like a tattling sister who has caught me red handed stealing cookies.

"No!" I shout back, "I have a home in Colorado!"

Her accusation is outlandish at best, but I don't need her undermining my relationship at the starting line. We stare at each other in silence for a few minutes before she turns away.

Just like that I watch her make herself at home in my girlfriend's apartment. Heels kicked under the coffee table she tucks her stocking covered feet underneath herself as she settles on the couch. She even fluffs my favorite pillow before settling against it. It's black with an orange cat silhouette that I find ridiculously charming.

"So, this is serious." Gabriella says from the kitchen where she has grabbed a pair of wine glasses.

She's not asking. She also isn't yelling like her friend, so I treat her statement like a question. One I take seriously.

"I want to marry her."

It's the first time I've said it out loud. Jill and Gabriella both turn to look at me with wide eyes, but

I don't care that it's barely been a couple of weeks. The words coat my feverish skin like a cool balm. This is right and it feels good to say it outright. Emma and I are meant for each other. Today, a week from now, or two years will make no difference. I know she's the one for me.

"You just met." Jill counters, voicing the concern that has plagued my mind since Colorado.

"That's why I haven't proposed." I explain, "And I need to get a ring."

I know we belong together, but I also know that Emma needs time. I can give her time. I just can't give her fifteen hundred miles of distance.

"This is crazy." Jill mutters as she accepts a glass of red wine from Gabriella.

"Love is crazy." Gabriella tells her as she sits down on the couch beside her.

They're looking at each other and not at me. I watch as eyebrows raise, and frowns turn into smiles. It's like the pair of them are carrying on a silent conversation which I am not privy to.

It's not something that would normally bother me. But since they knocked on the door, I have been the topic of conversation. My reasoning and my intentions. My very presence. And now I'm being left out of the conversation. One which could affect my relationship with Emma.

"I'm not a psycho. Not a serial killer. I just want to be

with Emma. Share our days with each other. I don't want to hear about what she had for lunch from fifteen hundred miles away. I want to hear it while we sit down for dinner. I love her."

"You love me?"

Emma

Andrew's shoulders tense under his faded blue shirt at my question. I can't see his face, but I can see over his shoulder the way Jill and Gabriella smirk at my interruption. Thanks to his work on the door, he didn't hear me come into the apartment until it was too late.

Turning his back on my friends, I'm startled by the look on his face. The determined set of his eyes looking at me with a vulnerable sort of hope combined with the way his mouth is set in a serious line. Neither smiling nor frowning. For the first time since we met, he looks nervous.

Out of his depth. Floundering with no grip on the outcome of this conversation, he looks worried.

I shouldn't be surprised to find my friends came over and cornered him without my knowledge. But I can't muster up the energy to be upset that they ignored my timeline, not when I came home to the best surprise. Even if I couldn't see the look on his face the first time he said those words. I heard them and felt their echo in my heart.

"I love you, Emma." He says. His blue eyes are dark with emotion. "I know it's crazy fast, I know you need time, but my heart doesn't beat without you near."

My words pile in my throat stealing the air from my lungs as my vision blurs. Every moment I've spent second guessing myself was in vain. Every step of the way this man was at my side. Not only physically but also emotionally.

As crazy as it may seem, we are on the same page. From that very first day we've been in sync.

"Andrew." I say between choked breaths. "It's not crazy. I love you too."

A single step is all it takes. I'm in Andrew's arms the fabric of his shirt soft against my cheek as his arms wrap around me and squeeze me tightly to his chest.

"Gag." Jill mutters to herself.

I hear the faint sound of Gabriella shushing her as Andrew rocks us back and forth. Without stepping away I wordlessly point at the door. Gabriella's giggles meld with Jill's quiet huffs of laughter as they leave. On the way out the door Jill slaps Andrew's back in farewell.

"Take care of our girl." Gabriella says just before they shut the door.

"I will." Andrew says to me, "Forever and ever I will."

Andrew

"Forgive me, Daddy for I've been naughty." Emma says as she presses her palms together and dips her head as if in prayer.

The beaded rosary wrapped around her right hand is a step further in this sacrilegious roleplay. I love the little details she's added to our costumes for this year's Halloween. It's been a week since we confessed our love for each other. I didn't think it could get any better but every day I swear I fall a little more in love with my Emma.

"Pray tell little one." I say, "What sins have you committed?"

I tip her chin up with my finger so that I can see her face. I'm seated on the bench seat at the end of our bed dressed as a priest, complete with cassock and cross.

"My dreams are filled with temptation." Emma says in a demure manner, "I dare not tell you the details or you shall think me wicked."

"I need to know the particulars so that I can decide your penance." I reply.

I stroke the side of her face gently with the back

of two fingers as she smiles timidly at me. She is kneeling in front of me dressed in a nun's habit complete with a veil that hides her hair from me and frames her face in white.

Such a pretty little bride of Christ my girlfriend makes.

"I cannot tell you." She says letting her gaze drop to the ground at my feet, "But perhaps I could show you."

I let her words hang for a moment, pretending to consider her proposition. Leaning down until our faces are an inch apart, I confess my own secret.

"You tempt me like no other. Use me to confess your own sin and make me guilty of yet another. I lust. I covet."

Her hands slide up my thighs. Closer and closer they creep to where my cock is sitting hard as granite. I reach down to pull her up until she is seated in my lap.

"If we must sin, and sin we must, let it be worth the penance."

I capture her lips with mine as she melts so sweetly against me. Every curve of her body pressing into me as my cock grows impossibly harder aching to be buried deep inside her until her wet warmth wraps around the length.

"Like this?" She asks as her fingers unbutton the fly front cape of my cassock.

"It's a start. Remember you are meant to show me the wickedness that tempts you, not the crosses of lustful burden I bare." I murmur as she removes my white collar and exposes my bare chest to her wandering hands.

Without warning she stands and begins to remove her habit. The veil remains as the rest of her outfit falls to the hardwood floor.

"Naughty little nun." I mutter as I take in her naked curves.

"Perverted priest." She retorts with a quiet laugh as she strokes a hand over my cloth covered cock.

"Be a good girl, Sister Emma." I say in a warning tone. "Penance can quickly become punishment."

"Oh, no." She says bringing her palm up to cover her open mouth in a blatant display of false shock. "Whatever will I do?"

"Apparently you'll be taking sacrament on your knees." I say standing up and letting my cassock fall to the floor, exposing the jutting length of my cock as I do.

Silently she sinks down, kneeling on the puddle of our clothing to cushion her knees. Her lips pop open without fanfare and I let out a shaky breath as she takes me in her mouth.

Her lips stretch wide as she takes me slowly. The curve of her tongue stroking the underside of my cock as I sink deeper into her wet mouth.

"Naughty." I groan as I sink into the hilt. Her mouth is so warm and wet and when she sucks on my length my knees nearly buckle.

My hands reach out to grab her hair, but my fingers find the stiff fabric of her veil instead. The mischievous glint in her eye is all the proof I need that she left it on to thwart me. She bobs her head twirling her tongue around the mushroom shaped head as she pulls away.

I rake my fingers through my own hair as Emma works my cock. Every muscle in my body is tense as she carries out her own form of punishment. As I feel my release draw closer, I step back pulling my cock out of her mouth in the process.

"Surely there is more?" I ask as I try to focus.

"You'll be so disappointed with me." She replies.

"Never." I say in a harsher tone than our little scene calls for and she knows it.

Her eyebrow rises in reproach, but she doesn't address the odd tone. The topic is too heavy for the moment and better ignored for now. I don't want her to ever think that she isn't everything I need. I can never be disappointed with her even in jest.

"Have I tempted you?" She asks as she stands.

I watch her slim fingers play with the end of her veil in a similar manner to the way she plays with her hair when she wants to appear coy.

"Always." I say breaking character once again as I

reach out to pull her body flush with mine.

Her skin is cool against mine. As she wraps her arms around my neck to pull me down for a kiss, I fall a little more in love with her. Ever since that first day we've just clicked. Not just sexually but in a truly meaningful way. Yes, the sex is off the charts but so is everything else.

We have no secrets, and no hidden shames. She accepts me just the way I am, and I accept her just the same. One day soon I'm going to get down on one knee and ask her to marry me. And I hope like hell she doesn't say it's too soon.

"Pray for our forgiveness." I order and wait for her to bring her palms together in front of her chest.

Bending down I grabbed the rosary that she dropped to the floor. Her eyes pop open as I begin wrapping the prayer beads around her wrists. The heat within her gaze is ratcheting up my own desire.

When I release her hands, she gives an experimental tug to test the knot. I watch as she moves each of her fingers before she gives the nod of approval. I grab her waist and toss her gently on the bed.

"Pray for our very souls." I whisper as I climb onto the bed between her thighs.

Emma eyes twinkle in the low light, the light green changing into the dark green of a placid lake with hidden depths. She murmurs a softly spoken prayer as I enter her swiftly, no mercy in my approach or my touch. Her hands strain against the rosary as she tries to touch me, but the bind holds. My rose covered hand pins hers above her head and with the veil in a white halo around her she looks every inch the virginal sacrifice.

Her moans sound like the sweetest prayer as I plunder her body. Nipples arching towards my mouth and thighs wrapping around my hips to pull me deeper she seeks control even as she lies helpless beneath me.

"Divine." I praise as her moans get higher in pitch and her walls begin to flutter around my length.

"Open wide, Sister Emma," I growl, "And receive my blessing."

On cue she clamps down on my cock, her muscles milking me as she comes around my cock. Eyes rolling back as she arches her back, every muscle in her body tenses as she cries out.

Thrusting steadily, I don't let up, watching her fall apart under me, as I continue to hammer my hips into hers. Grinding my teeth I try in vain to hold back, but when she hooks her ankles behind my back and peers up at me from under her eyelashes I spiral out of control.

"Give it to me." She pleads, her full lips parted and her eyes soft, "Come for me, Babe."

Helpless to resist I come with her name whispered on my lips as she takes every drop of my seed with a lusty smile on her face.

"Best Halloween, ever." She says later while we lie cuddled together.

"Yet." I correct with a gentle pat to her ass, "I'm already planning for next year."

Her soft laughter lulls me to a languid state before I drift off to sleep, the gentle press of her lips to my jaw the last thing I remember before darkness takes me.

Epilogue

Emma

Six Months Later

Forty minutes into our hike, Andrew tugs me to an overlook. The trail we're on is coated in pine needles and tall grass grows between towering trees on both sides. It's not the most picturesque trail we've explored in Georgia but the view at the top of the mountain is supposed to be stunning.

Sweaty with my tank top sticking to my back, I'm happy for a respite. It may be April but it's already gearing up to be a scorching summer. Today more than any other I'm glad I moved to Colorado with Andrew. It might have its downsides, but I prefer the snow to the blazing heat and the solitude of our cabin compared to my old apartment.

We're back visiting family and friends. Andrew made a smashing impression on my family all those months ago. My own brother claims Andrew will get him if we ever breakup. The jerk.

Panting to catch my breath, I step onto the grass covered cliff looking down at the mountain range around us and the sea of trees covering them so that they look like green waves.

"It's pretty." I say to Andrew.

He picked this trail, and I don't want him to think I'm disappointed with his selection. There's no one around for miles and we only have the chirping birds and squirrels for company out here. Other trails may have better vistas, but I like the break in our trip.

We've been surrounded by people all week. Dinners and game nights as we try to pack in as much time with everyone as possible before we leave for home. When Andrew doesn't respond right away, I turn to look at him and find him kneeling behind me with an open ring box clutched between fingers turning white at the tips.

"Emma," He begins before pausing, every emotion visible in his eyes as he takes a deep breath and audibly swallows.

"Will you marry me?" He asks.

For a moment we're frozen in time. I can feel every beat of my heart pounding like a bass drum. It's like forgetting how to breathe as tears fill my eyes and I nod rapidly choking on my answer.

"Yes." I manage to say between breaths.

Our bodies collide a moment later, my arms wrapping around his neck and pulling him down for a kiss that starts sweet and ends utterly filthy.

"It will be a lengthy engagement." I tell him after we

break apart.

His lips are red from my nibbles, and I love the slightly drunk look that he always gets after we kiss.

"In case you change your mind?" He asks with a cheeky grin.

"No!" I say slapping his chest, "To plan the perfect wedding."

"And honeymoon." Andrew adds and I can't resist rolling my eyes.

"Of course." I nod before I see a mischievous glint sparkle in his eye.

This late in the afternoon and this trail is empty of people. I'm sure that's why Andrew picked this one instead of another in this national park.

"Run." He growls, "I'm going to chase you and when I catch you, I'm going to breed your sweet little pussy raw."

I spin on my heel and begin running back down the mountain. The path is packed dirt that slides underneath my tennis shoes, but I make good progress. Faster than running up the trail, I'd be out of breath before I reached the next overlook. I hear Andrew's heavy footsteps behind me louder than the heartbeat pounding in my ears. Stronger and faster, he closes in fast before letting me slip away at the last second.

I'm panting with exertion but he's not even slightly winded as he darts in close again. The way he toys with me only excites me as he makes a playful grab for my arm. Then as we pass a bend in the trail, he makes his move.

One moment I'm running down the trail and the next he has whisked me off my feet. Ignoring my fists beating onto his back he carries me into a clearing.

"Too slow." Andrew growls into my ear as he sets me down, "Did you really think you could escape me?"

I try to stand but a quick yank on my ankle has me sprawled out beneath him again. Wordlessly he uses his hold on my leg to flip me over onto my stomach.

"I'll do anything-" I begin to plead when Andrew shoves my head down to the forest floor.

Wet leaves stick to my face as I hear the clink of Andrew's belt buckle as it hits the ground.

"You'll do nothing." He says, "You'll lie down and take my cock like the pretty little prey you are."

"Or what?" I ask as his hands wrench my leggings down to my knees where he leaves them.

"Or nothing." He growls. "You're mine to fuck as I please."

I can't help the moan that slips out of my mouth as he squeezes my ass in a punishing grip.

"I'm going to fuck this cunt until it is swollen and dripping with my seed."

His fingers stroke over my damp panties as I bite my

lips to keep quiet.

"Dirty little girl." He purrs as he teases my outer lips through the underwear. "You're wet just from thinking about my cock plowing into your juicy little pussy."

The strike comes out of nowhere. His hand slapping my pussy with enough force to sting, causing me to yelp.

"Naughty." He says.

My damp panties briefly cling to my skin as he peels them down to join my leggings.

"Look at this pretty little cunt, already dripping for my cock." He runs a rough finger lightly through my folds just teasing my entrance without entering.

His hand wraps in my hair using his grip on the strands to pull my head up. My scalp stinging from the rough yank, my vision goes blurry with tears.

"Beg for it." He snarls with his chin resting on my shoulder.

Seated like we are the head of his cock is nudging my entrance. I wiggle backwards trying to tempt him into plunging his length inside me.

"*Beg*." He orders giving my hair a sharp tug in reproach, his voice a deep rumble that sends a fluttering pulse deep inside my core.

I want to deny him. See how far I can push him until he breaks. The sharp sting of his hand striking my ass has me reconsidering.

"Please." I say in my sweetest voice.

The hand in my hair twists tighter until the tingling of my scalp is bordering on true pain.

"Please. What." He bites out his breath hot on my ear.

"Please fuck me." I cry. "Fuck me like the dirty whore I am."

"Good girl." He croons before he nudges the head of his cock into my entrance.

I almost scream with frustration when he stops. The hand wrapped around his cock that's sandwiched between his thigh and my ass pulls away.

"Andrew." I plead as his hands grab my hips, the pads of his fingers biting into my flesh with a brutal grip.

He doesn't respond. Without warning he uses his hold on me to slam my hips down. His cock plunges into me fully to the hilt in one stroke. His grip controls my body raising and slamming me back down on his cock while I try to help. The wet squelch of our bodies meeting only grows louder as he works me on his length.

I come apart screaming his name, startling a nearby flock of birds that leap into flight cawing their reproach.

He pauses long enough to reach around and grab my throat with a firm hand.

"Feeling good Emma?" He asks in a mocking tone,

"Was that good for you?"

I nod enthusiastically trying to steady my breathing between gasps.

"How lovely." He purrs squeezing my throat for a moment as he licks my cheek. "I'm so happy that was good for *you*."

His hand releases my throat, and I draw in a shaky breath. The muscles in my legs tremble as he runs a rough hand along the inside of my thigh. His fingers find my clit, his touch slick from my arousal as he pinches the sensitive nub between his thumb and finger.

"Ah." I gasp my back arching as he pinches it twice, the second press of his fingers lingering longer.

The pain fades leaving a warm feeling of awareness behind as Andrew reaches between us to press a strong palm to my back. I bend over, my hot face returning to the leaf covered ground.

Andrew shifts to his knees, even the small adjustment causing his cock to move inside me drawing a soft moan from my lips.

"I'll never get tired of seeing how this wet little pussy looks wrapped around my cock." He says as he pulls away before thrusting back into me.

"Mine. Say it." He growls as he pulls away, almost his entire length leaving me as he plants a foot beside my knees.

The next thrust goes impossibly deeper as his grip

on my hips turns bruising.

"*Mine.*" He snarls, his word a claiming and an order.

"Yours." I cry as he hammers his cock into me.

He pays no attention to my cries as he drives his hips into mine over and over. I come on his cock screaming his name with my muscles clenching and trying to lock him in place.

Paying me no heed his pace remains consistent, not allowing me to come down from one orgasm before he sends me spiraling into another.

"Emma. Fuck." He groans as his hips stutter to a halt, his fingers squeezing my sides as he comes coating my walls with sticky warm seed.

He pulls back his limp cock dangling as we both right our clothes. With dirt on my hands and knees I know I look a fright, but nothing can wipe the satisfied grin from my face.

"Love you my pretty little wife to be." Andrew says just before he kisses me.

Bonus Epilogue

Emma

Three Years Later

"Beautiful day for a wedding." Andrew says as we take our seats next to Gabriella and Oliver. Gabriella is six months pregnant with a swollen belly that enters the room before she does, and Oliver is beside himself with worry anytime she's on her feet for more than five minutes.

"Still can't believe Jill didn't want any kind of wedding party." Oliver mutters to himself as much as us.

"She's always been independent." Gabriella says before adding as she gestures to her stomach, "I'm just glad I don't have to fit all of this into chaffron and tulle."

"Does he mean to look so arrogant?" Andrew murmurs to me eyes fixed ahead on the man standing beside the priest.

I can't argue that Alan does look a tad arrogant. I'm not sure if it's the smirk or his posture that screams superiority, but I suspect it's both.

"Yes." I reply, "He and Jill are a perfect match."

"I was happy to see her taken down a few pegs." He confides in a whisper that makes Oliver chuckle.

"Karma." He agrees.

"Shush. The pair of you I swear! They are a wonderful couple." I chide in a whisper mindful of the people seated around us.

"You made me wait an eternity." Andrew complains, "They've been engaged a month."

"Less than two years after you proposed we got married." I reply, "And our wedding was worth the wait."

Andrew's soft smile is the only agreement I need. He remembers our wedding day as fondly as I do. The pre-ceremony fuck in the dressing room. The lace dress that he peeled off my body later that night. And then the honeymoon that Andrew planned for us in the Caribbean.

"I would have worn the blue tux if you had agreed to an elopement." Andrew says right before the wedding march begins playing.

I turn to give him a frosty glare to find him grinning from ear to ear. I know he's trying to fire me up. I know all his tricks at this point but damn me if they don't still work.

The devilish bastard was perfectly agreeable on everything except for two things. The cake flavor and his attire. I tried for months to convince him to wear a navy blue tux that I thought he would look delicious in. In the end the cake was red velvet with cream cheese frosting, and he wore a black suit with a blue tie.

I'll die before I admit that the tux wouldn't have looked as good as the suit. He knows that I know it. But I won't give him the satisfaction of telling him so. His tattooed hand grabs mine, the floral bouquet on my skin blending beautifully with his roses as we stand to watch Jill walk down the aisle on the arm of Alan's dad.

For now, we'll be proper but later I'm going to tie him to the bed and fuck that attitude out of him. He'll shut up and take that strap on like a good boy if I have anything to say about it.

Author Note

Thanks for reading *Pumpkin Spiced Love!* If you liked, loved, loathed, or hated it please leave an honest review or rating. They help my books find the right audience (Yes even the negative ones) and make all the difference to indie authors like me.

I don't send newsletters, and I don't have a website so if you want to be notified about any new releases you can follow me on Amazon.

I had a blast writing Emma and Andrew's love story. What started out as a spicy short quickly grew into something far bigger. Originally, I had planned to publish this story in line with my Crescent Ridge Mail Order Brides series and title it *Mountain Man's Filthy Love*. I liked the title because my spiciest romance to date was *Mountain Man's Dirty Mail Order Bride*. But while they share the same world and a good chunk of the story does take place in Crescent Ridge, Emma could never be a mail order bride. Although she is very impulsive.

Finishing the story PSL clearly belongs with the other Holiday Sweet Treats. I don't know why I ever considered putting it anywhere else. Sometime in the near future I plan to replace the covers for the ebooks, if only to make it clear they are steamy. Then I'll set up paperbacks for *Sweetheart* and *Pumpkin Spiced Love* using the old covers. Maybe with a few tweaks. I don't *love* the last two covers. I designed all three myself but *Cinnamon Kissed* is the only one I feel a true affinity for. Thankfully, I chose to be a writer and not a graphic designer.

Next up I'm working on more mountain man romances including two men in uniform. After that I have another Monster Merge romance in the works. And then I am tempted to dabble in sci-fi romance. But that is off in the far future. I have at least five novellas to finish before I even consider another project.

Thanks again for reading and I hope to see you in the next one!

Books In This Series

Holiday Sweet Treats

Cinnamon Kissed

Sweetheart

Crescent Ridge Mail Order Brides

Mountain Man's Modern Mail Order Bride
Mountain Man's Rescued Mail Order Bride
Mountain Man's Rejected Mail Order Bride
Mountain Man's Dirty Mail Order Bride
Reclusive Mountain Man's Mail Order Bride
Mountain Man's Stolen Mail Order Bride
Mountain Man's Sweet Mail Order Bride

Crescent Ridge: Mountain Men In Uniform

A Bride For Thomas
A Bride For Scott
A Bride For Dennis

Pearl's Modern Mail Order Brides

The Lighthouse Keeper's Mail Order Bride

Pearl's Mail Order Brides

The First Mountain Man's Mail Order Bride
The Outlaw Mountain Man's Mail Order Bride
The Texan's Matchmaking Bride

Monster Merge

Goblin Hunt
My Orcish Mate
Faerie Tale
Orc Me Crazy

Standalones

Dr. Ghoul's Girl
Ensorcelled

About The Author

Jacqueline Carmine

A southern transplant in Michigan, Jacqueline spends most of winter indoors writing about monsters, men, and the women who love them. She prefers insta-love over slow burn but loves a good groveling scene. She drinks energy drinks daily to keep up with her husband and three dogs and has never refused a good tiramisu. She adores all dogs, most cats, and plants that actually want to live.

Manufactured by Amazon.ca
Acheson, AB